Hector
the Horrid Hopper

Based on *The Railway Series* by the Rev. W. Awdry

Illustrations by *Robin Davies*

EGMONT

EGMONT

We bring stories to life

First published in Great Britain 2008
This edition published in 2011
by Egmont UK Limited
The Yellow Building, 1 Nicholas Road, London, W11 4AN

Thomas the Tank Engine & Friends™

CREATED BY BRITT ALLCROFT

Based on the Railway Series by the Reverend W Awdry
© 2011 Gullane (Thomas) LLC. A HIT Entertainment company.
Thomas the Tank Engine & Friends and Thomas & Friends are trademarks of Gullane (Thomas) Limited.
Thomas the Tank Engine & Friends and Design is Reg. U.S. Pat. & Tm. Off.

HiT entertainment

ISBN 978 1 4052 69735
45463/8
Printed in Italy

Stay safe online. Egmont is not responsible for content hosted by third parties.

FSC
MIX
Paper
FSC® C018306

Egmont is passionate about helping to preserve the world's remaining ancient forests.
We only use paper from legal and sustainable forest sources.

This book is made from paper certified by the Forest Stewardship Council® (FSC®),
an organisation dedicated to promoting responsible management of forest resources.
For more information on the FSC, please visit www.fsc.org. To learn more about
Egmont's sustainable paper policy, please visit www.egmont.co.uk/ethical

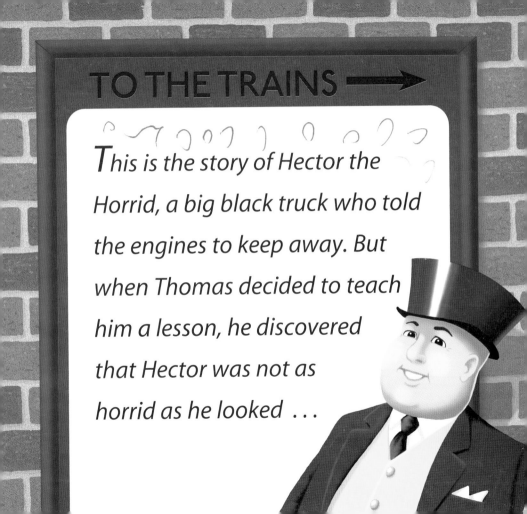

This is the story of Hector the Horrid, a big black truck who told the engines to keep away. But when Thomas decided to teach him a lesson, he discovered that Hector was not as horrid as he looked ...

Thomas the Tank Engine loves shunting Troublesome Trucks.

He can biff them harder and faster than any other engine.

It's one of his favourite jobs.

One morning, The Fat Controller had an important announcement.

"James and Edward must take extra deliveries of coal," he boomed.

"Thomas, you must shunt and fill trucks at the Coaling Plant for James and Edward to collect this afternoon," he added.

Thomas was very pleased.

Just then, Bill and Ben chuffed by with a big, black truck. It was biffing and bashing them.

"*Two* engines pushing *one* truck?" said Thomas.

"This is Hector," huffed Bill. "He hates being shunted. We call him Hector the Horrid!"

Bill and Ben chuffed slowly away with Hector.

"I could biff Hector firmly into place," Thomas boasted to James.

Later, Thomas chuffed into the Coaling Plant. And there was Hector.

The other trucks giggled. *"Big, bad and solid, he's Hector the Horrid*!" they sang.

Thomas puffed closer.

"KEEP AWAY!" roared Hector.

"Bill and Ben were right," thought Thomas, "Hector *is* horrid!"

Thomas decided to keep away. He spent the morning shunting the other trucks and filling them with coal.

All the time, Thomas could feel Hector the Horrid watching him.

The Plant Manager came to see Thomas. "We need an extra large delivery," he said. "You must shunt and fill Hector. Rosie is coming to help."

Later, Rosie puffed into the yard. She saw Hector. "Do we have to shunt that big truck, Thomas?" she peeped.

"Yes," puffed Thomas. "But he doesn't want to be shunted! His name is . . ."

Before Thomas could finish, Hector opened his mouth and let out the biggest roar ever!

"KEEP AWAY!" he bellowed.

Rosie was so surprised that she shook from funnel to footplate, and steamed straight out of the yard!

This made Thomas cross.

Hector had biffed and bashed Bill and Ben . . . He had shouted at Thomas . . . And frightened Rosie so much, that she had puffed away.

Now the extra delivery would never be ready!

Thomas had had enough! He puffed up to Hector . . . and biffed him!

Hector was cross. "KEEP AWAY!" he roared.

"I won't!" huffed Thomas. "You are causing confusion and delay! You really are horrid!"

Then with one mighty biff, Thomas pushed Hector backwards into a set of buffers. Hector couldn't stop, and rolled right off the track!

Thomas felt very bad. He hadn't meant to biff Hector so hard! He puffed over to the truck.

Hector lay on his side, looking very sad. Now Hector didn't seem so horrid.

"I'm sorry I biffed you so hard," wheeshed Thomas. "But why won't you be shunted?"

"I'm scared!" moaned Hector.

Thomas was surprised.

"I'm a new truck," Hector groaned. "I'm scared of being filled with coal. I've never done it before. That's why I didn't want to be shunted."

Thomas wanted to help Hector. "Sometimes I'm scared when I have to do something new," Thomas chuffed, "but coal isn't scary!"

Later, Rocky arrived. He lifted Hector back on to the tracks.

Hector watched Thomas roll under the hopper. Black, dusty coal poured into Thomas' coal box.

"See, it's not scary," Thomas peeped, kindly.

Then Hector smiled. "I'd like to be filled with coal, too," he rumbled.

So Thomas pulled Hector quickly under the hopper to fill him up with coal.

Thomas shunted Hector into place, just as James and Edward puffed into the yard.

They were surprised to see Hector there.

Soon, the trains were ready, and James and Edward puffed away to make their deliveries.

"Good luck!" Thomas whistled.

But the whistle wasn't for them. Thomas was tooting to his new friend, Hector, who wasn't horrid, after all!